Toot & Puddle

by

Holly Hobbie

LITTLE, BROWN AND COMPANY

New York ᴥ Boston

Little, Brown and Company

Time Warner Book Group
1271 Avenue of the Americas, New York, NY 10020
Visit our Web site at www.lb-kids.com

First Edition

Library of Congress Cataloging-in-Publication Data

Hobbie, Holly
    Toot and Puddle / by Holly Hobbie. — 1st ed.
        p.   cm.
    Summary: Toot and Puddle are best friends with very different
interests, so when Toot spends the year traveling around the world,
Puddle enjoys receiving his postcards.
    ISBN 0-316-36552-1
    [1. Pigs — Fiction.   2. Travel — Fiction.   3. Friendship — Fiction.
4. Postcards — Fiction.]   I. Title.
PZ7.H6515Ad   1997
[E] — dc20   96-28649

10

SC

Manufactured in China

The paintings for this book were done in watercolor

Toot and Puddle lived together in Woodcock Pocket.

It was such a perfect place to be that Puddle never wanted to go anywhere else.

Toot, on the other hand, loved to take trips. He had been to Cape Cod, the Grand Canyon, and the redwood forests.

One day in January, Toot decided to set off on his biggest trip ever.
He decided to see the world. "Do you want to come along?" he asked
Puddle. "We could start with someplace warm and wild."

 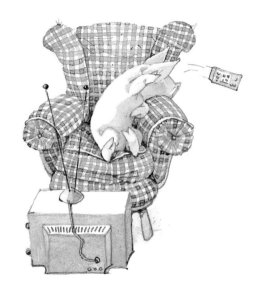 

Puddle preferred to stay home.

I love snow, he thought.

Meanwhile...presenting Puddle at Pocket Pond!

MARCH ON THE NILE

Dear Puddle,
    EGYPT is Awesome.
The Pyramids are
the greatest. Wish
You COULD MEET me
at the Oasis.
    Your Friend,
        TooT

To: Puddle
Woodcock Pocket
    U.S.A.

PAR AVION

MARCH
RIVER
PM
NILE

EGYPT

March meant maple syrup. Puddle wished Toot were there to taste the pancakes.

Dear Puddle,
Can you believe I'm
in the Solomon Islands?
They're in the Pacific
Ocean. I spend all day
underwater. I love
being in a school —
of fish. Has Spring
come yet?
Your pal,
Toot.

APRIL
SOLOMON ISLANDS
AM

Puddle
Woodcock Pocket
U.S.A.

SOLOMON ISLANDS

Yes, spring had arrived. Puddle was having mud season. Yay!

Back at Woodcock Pocket...
"For he's a jolly good fellow,
for he's a jolly good fellow,
for he's a jolly good fellow,
that nobody can deny!"

Puddle remembered.

In July…presenting Puddle at Pocket Pond! Every
time he jumped in, he cheered, *"Olé!"*

Dear Puddle,
    August is cold in
Antarctica, but I've
made more friends
here than anywhere
yet. Are you going
to the beach this
year? I miss you.
Do you miss me?
    Friends Forever,
        Toot

To: Puddle
WOODCOCK POCKET
U.S.A.

SOUTH POLE
SOUTH GEORGIA PM
AUGUST

Yes, Puddle missed his friend.

Dear Pudsy,
Bonjour from Paris,
Art is everywhere!
Love is in the air!
Au revoir,
Toot

To:
Puddle
Woodcock Pocket
U.S.A.

I love art, thought Puddle.

Dearest Pudsio,
Italy is heaven—
it's one big treat!
Your friend,
Tootsio

To:
Puddle
Woodcock Pocket
U.S.A.

OCTOBER
AM
FLORENCE ITALY

ITALY

VIA AERIA

Meanwhile, it was Halloween in Woodcock Pocket.

Puddle decided to be horrifying.

One morning in November, Toot woke up and thought, *It's time to go home.*

Yay, Toot's coming!

December called for celebration.
"Here's to all your adventures around the world," said Puddle.
"Here's to all your adventures right at home," said Toot.

"And here's to being together again," Toot and Puddle
said at the same time.

Toot was happy to be back in his own bed, and
Puddle was happy, too.

"I wonder if it will snow all night," Puddle said.
"I hope so," said Toot.
"Then we'll go sliding," said Puddle.
"And skiing," said Toot.
"Good night, Toot."
"Good night, Puddle."

JP   Hobbie, Holly.

         Toot & Puddle.

DATE			